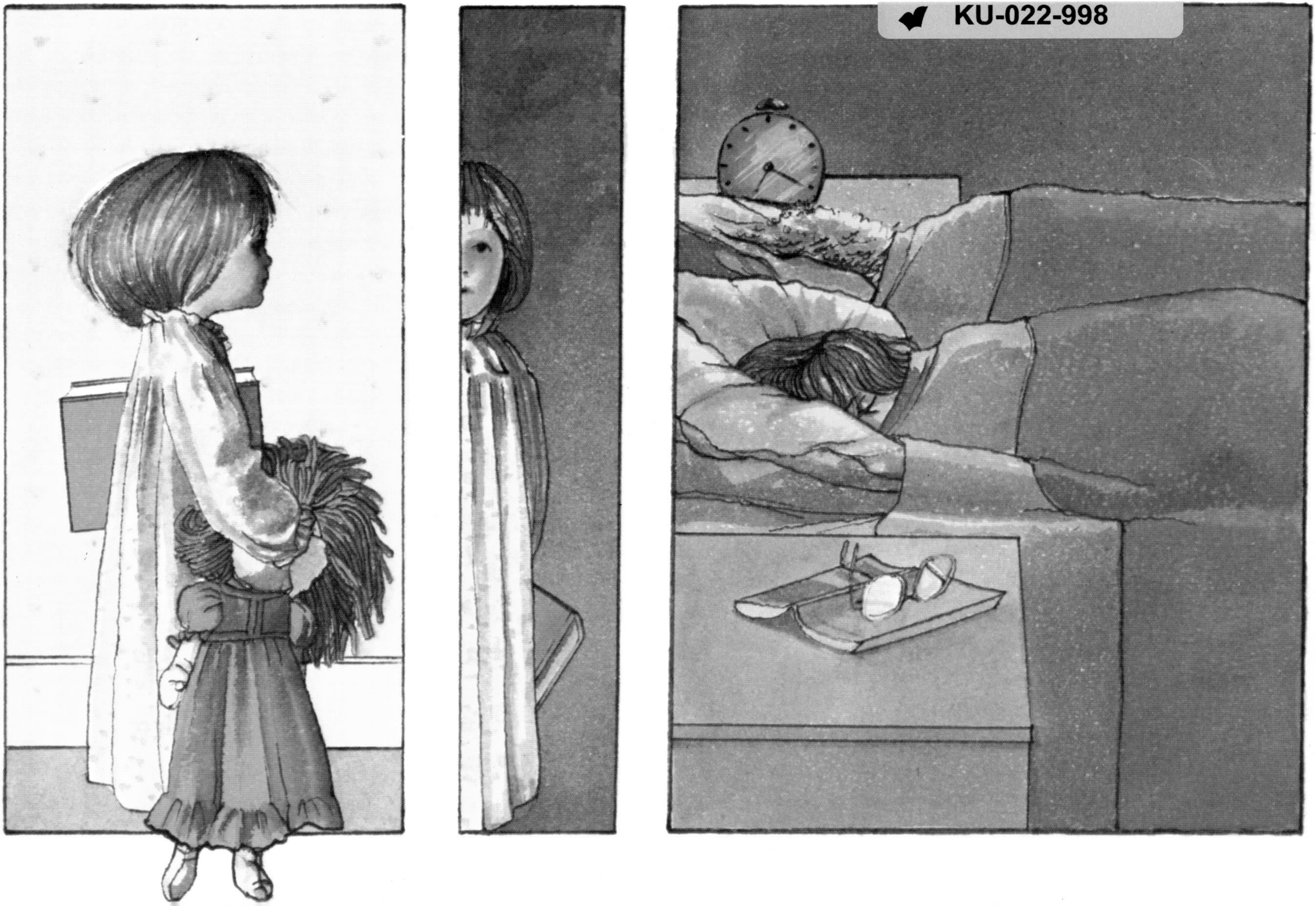

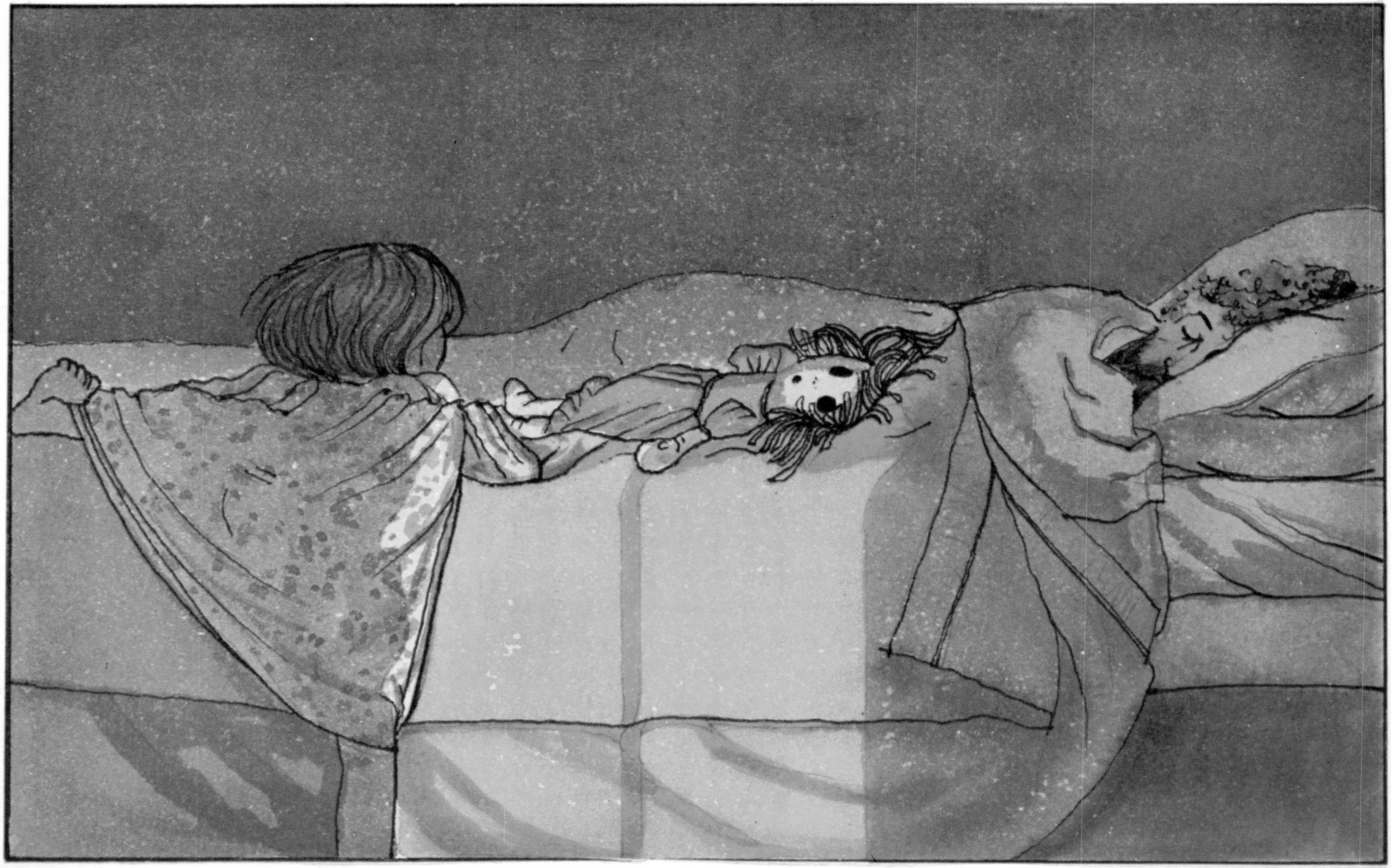

Jan Ormerod

Sunshine

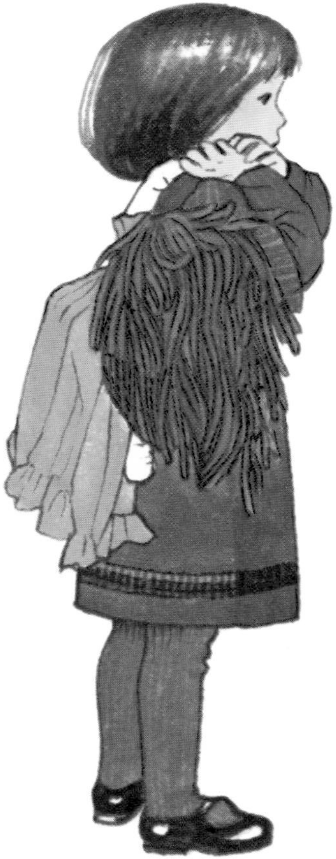

VIKING

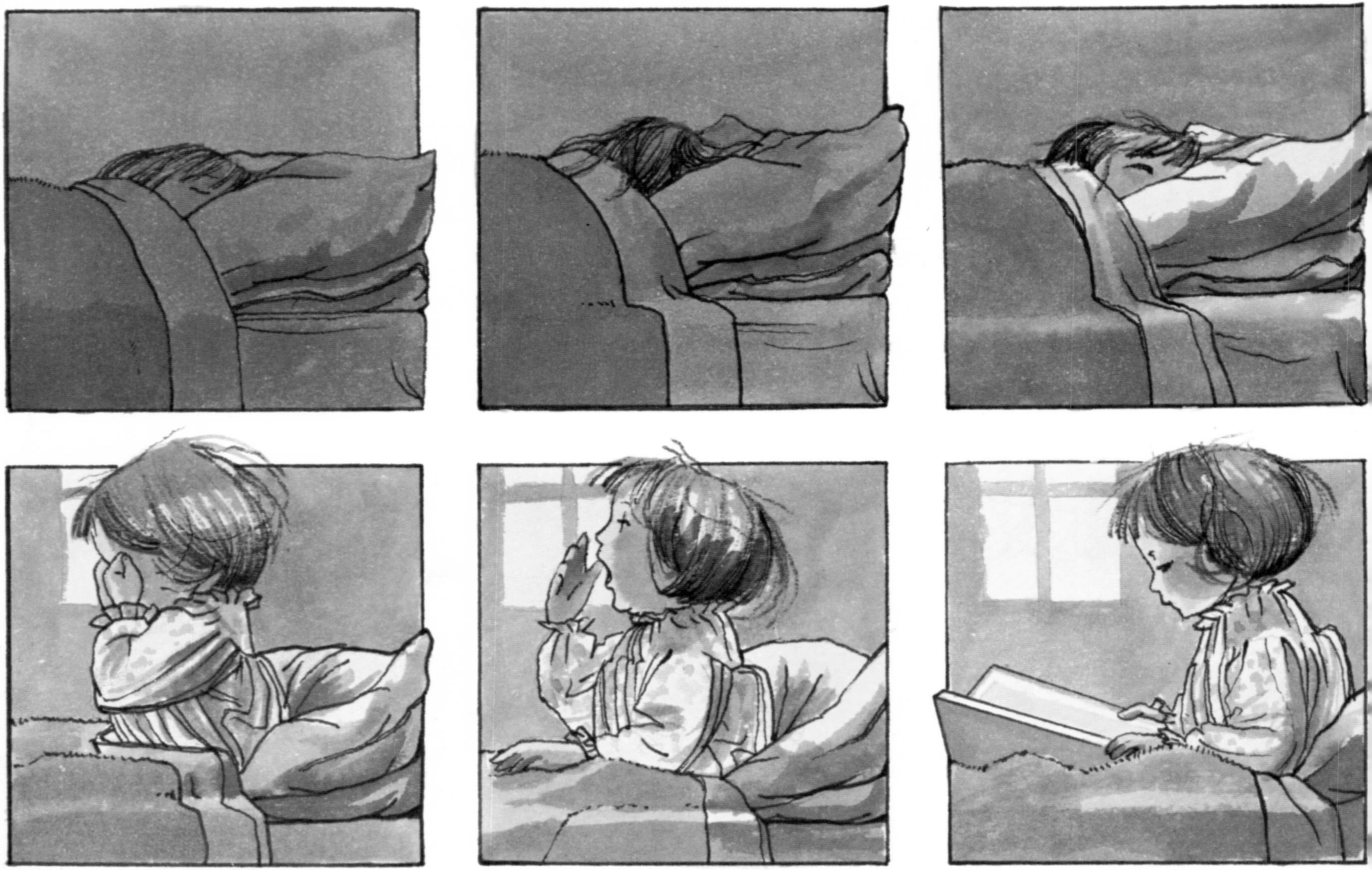

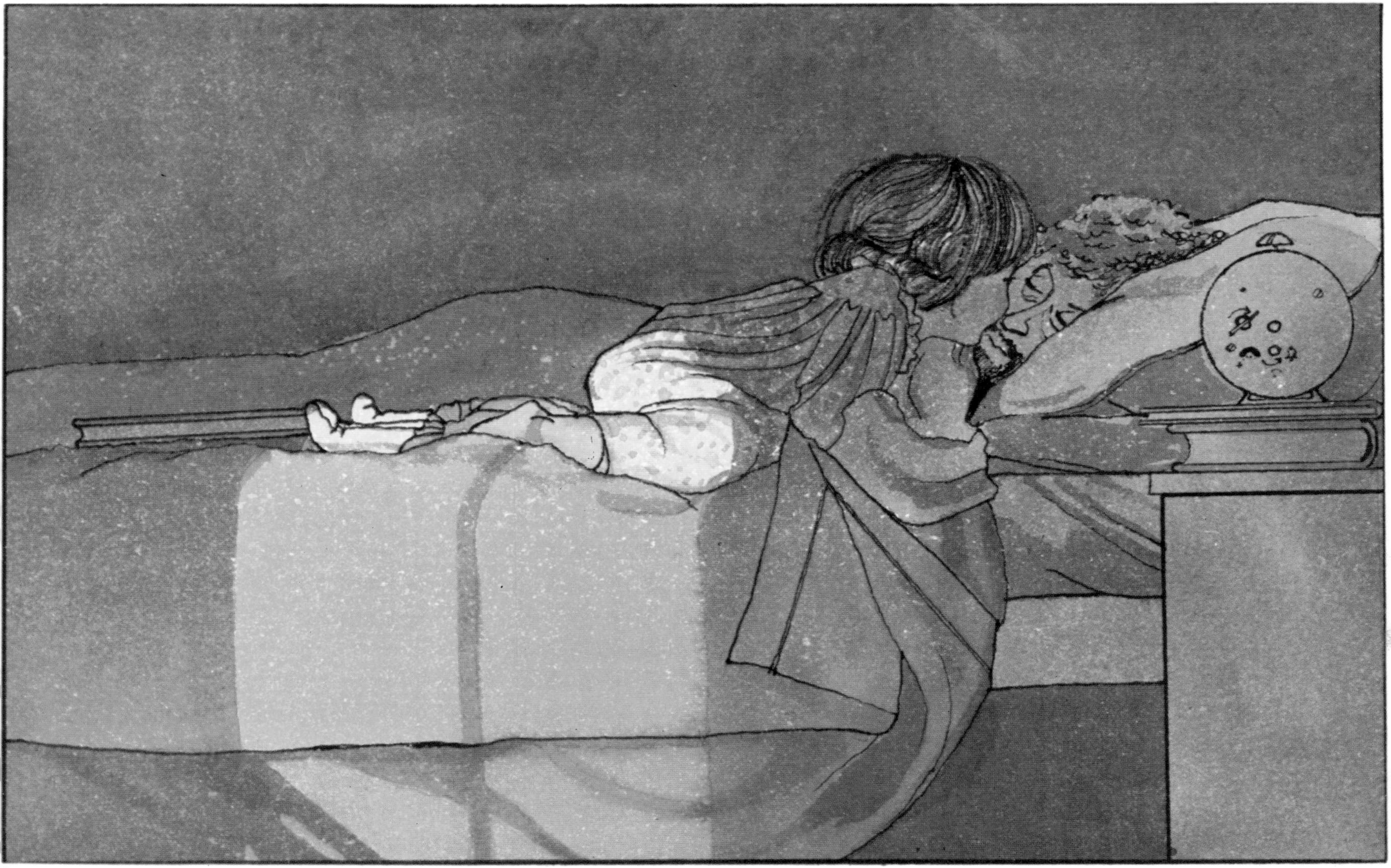

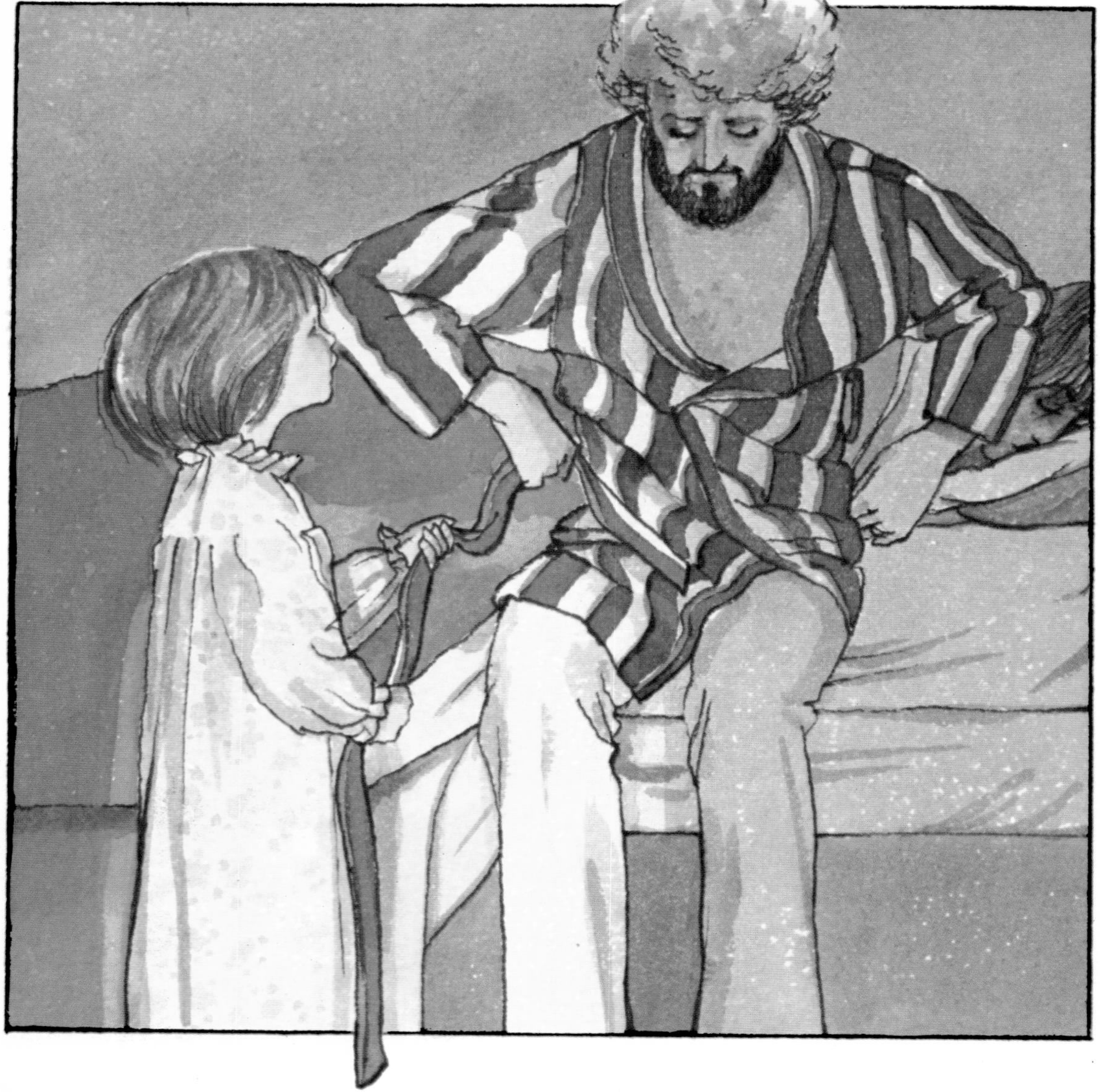
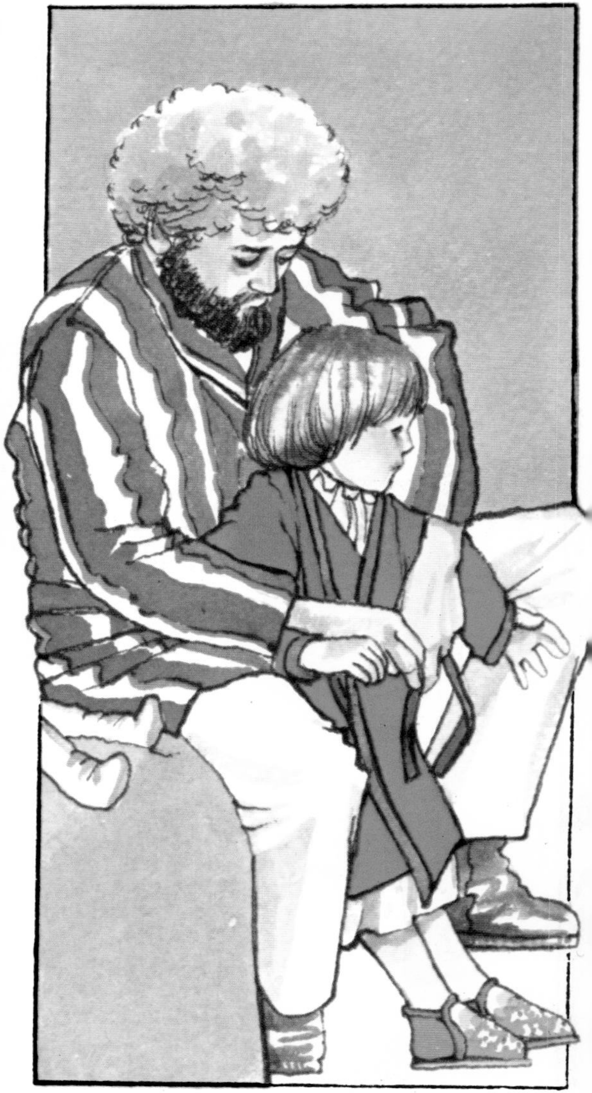

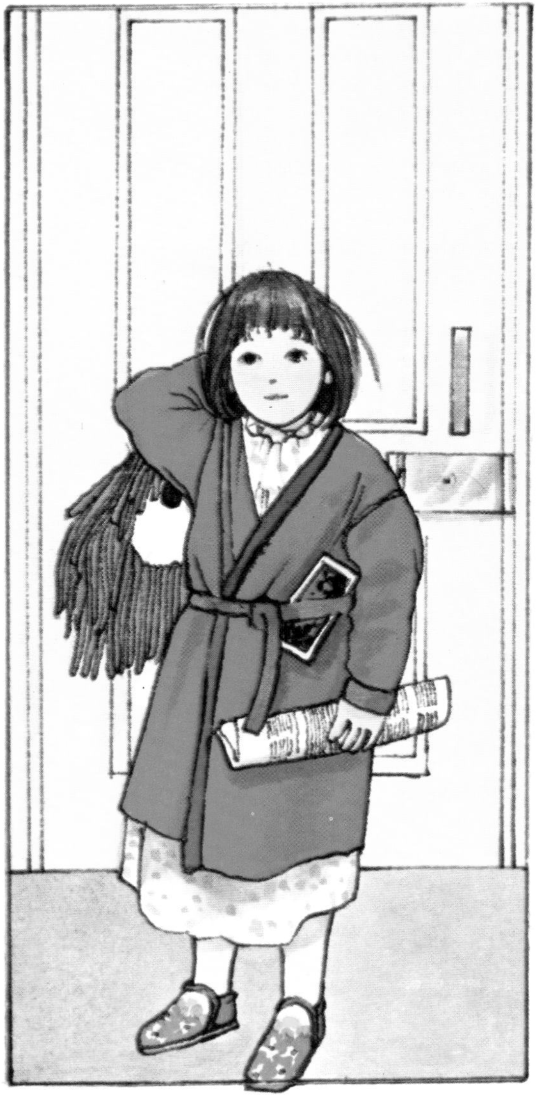
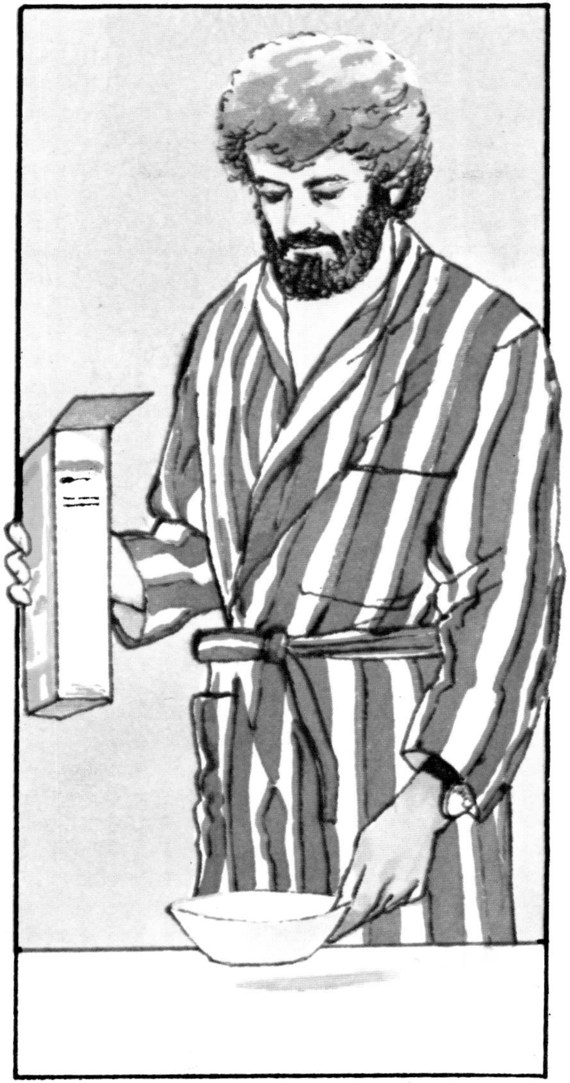
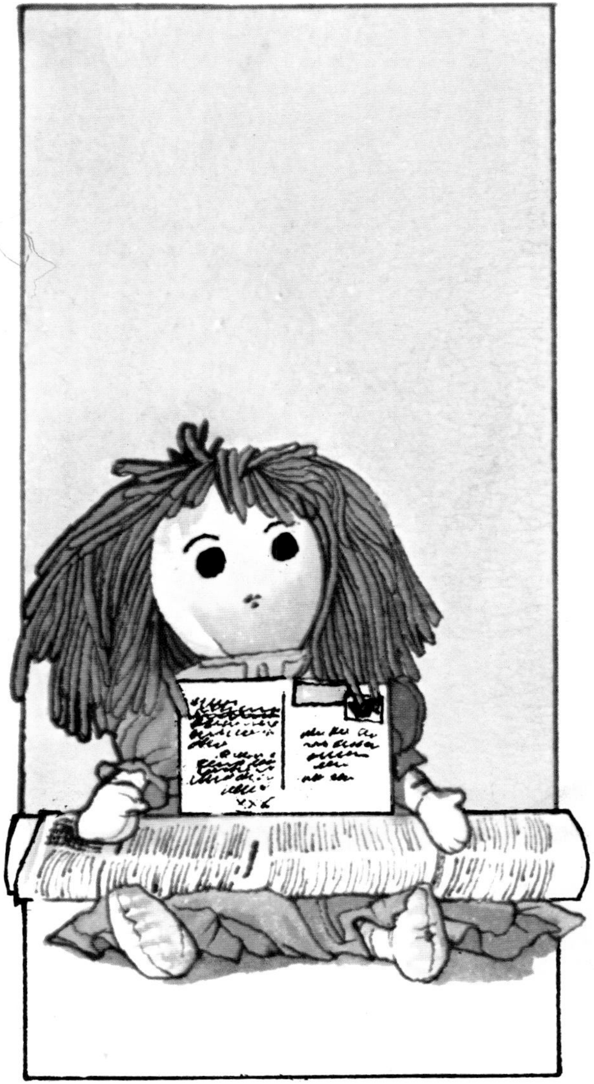

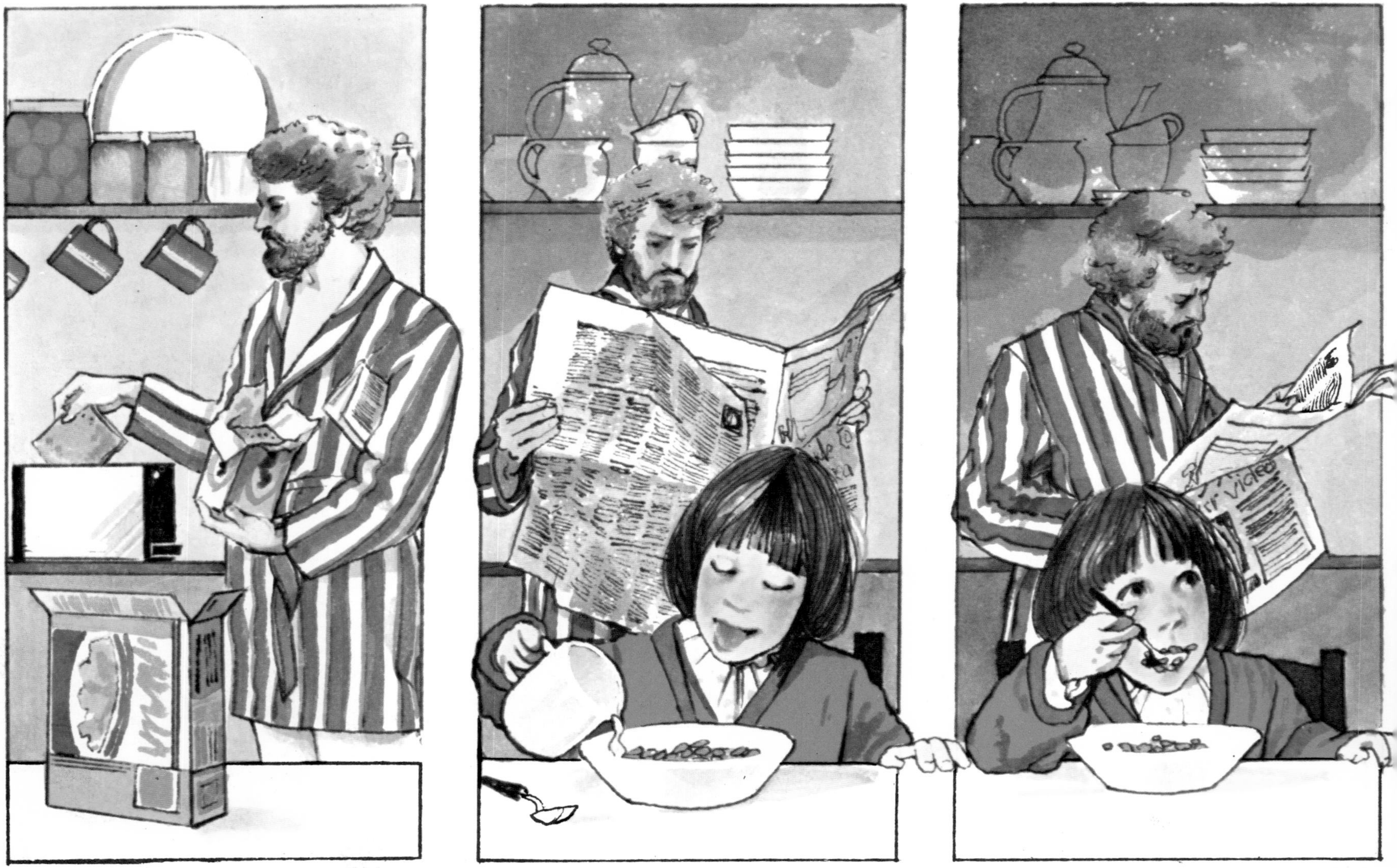

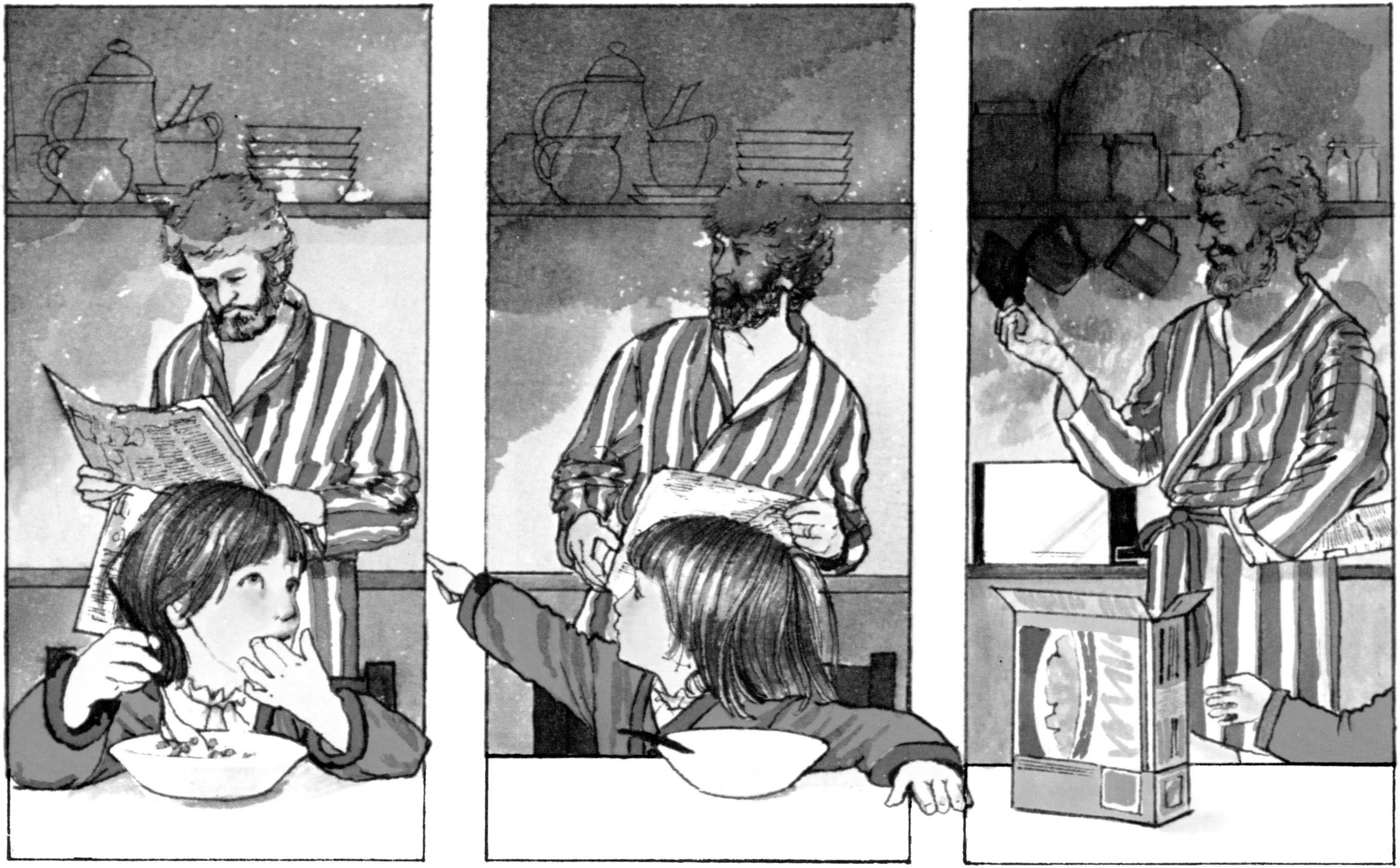

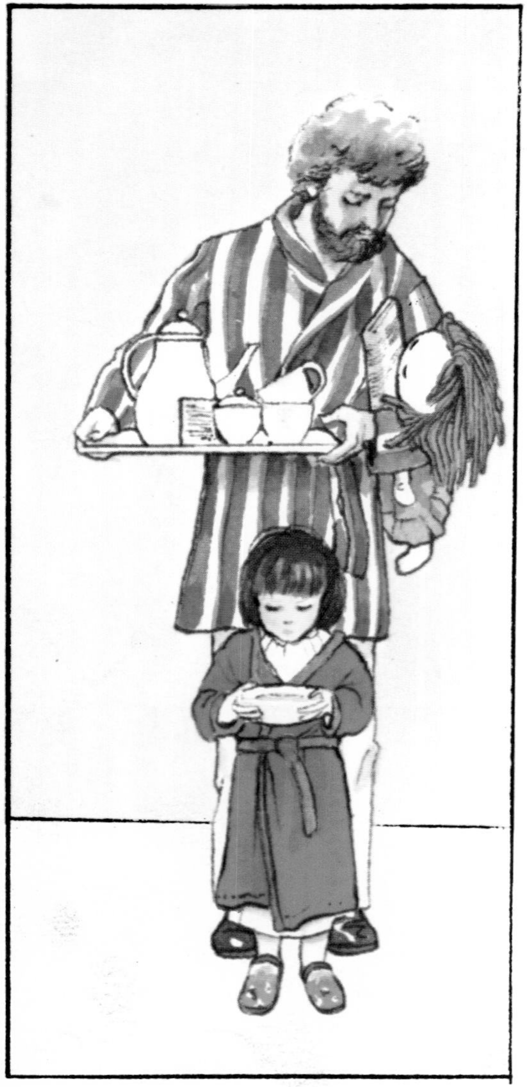
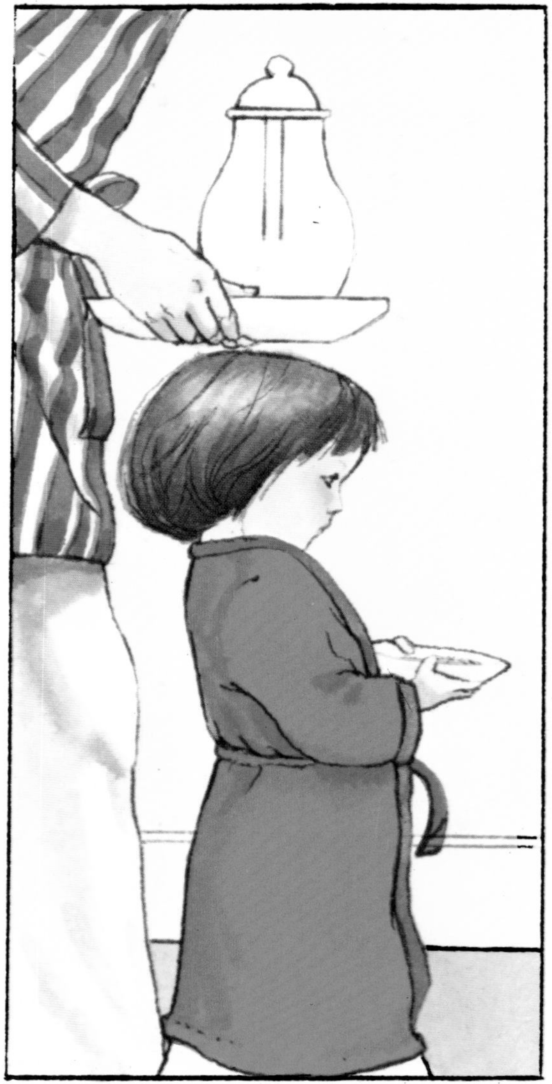
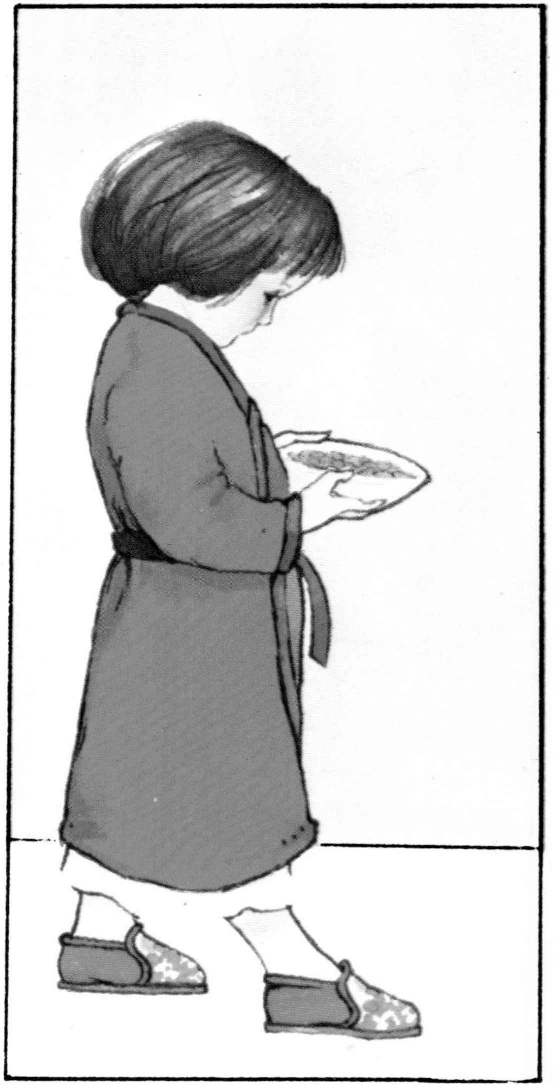

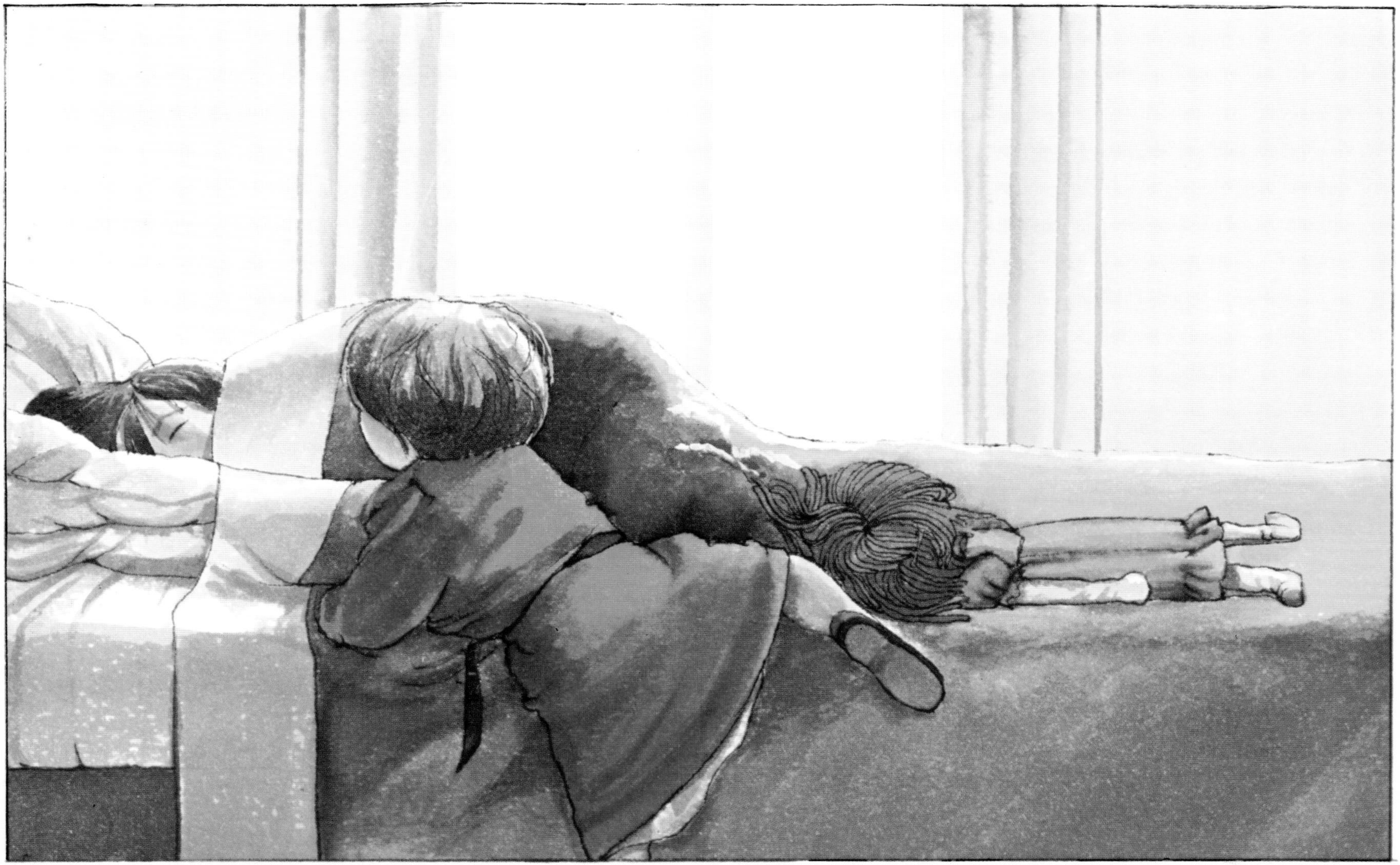

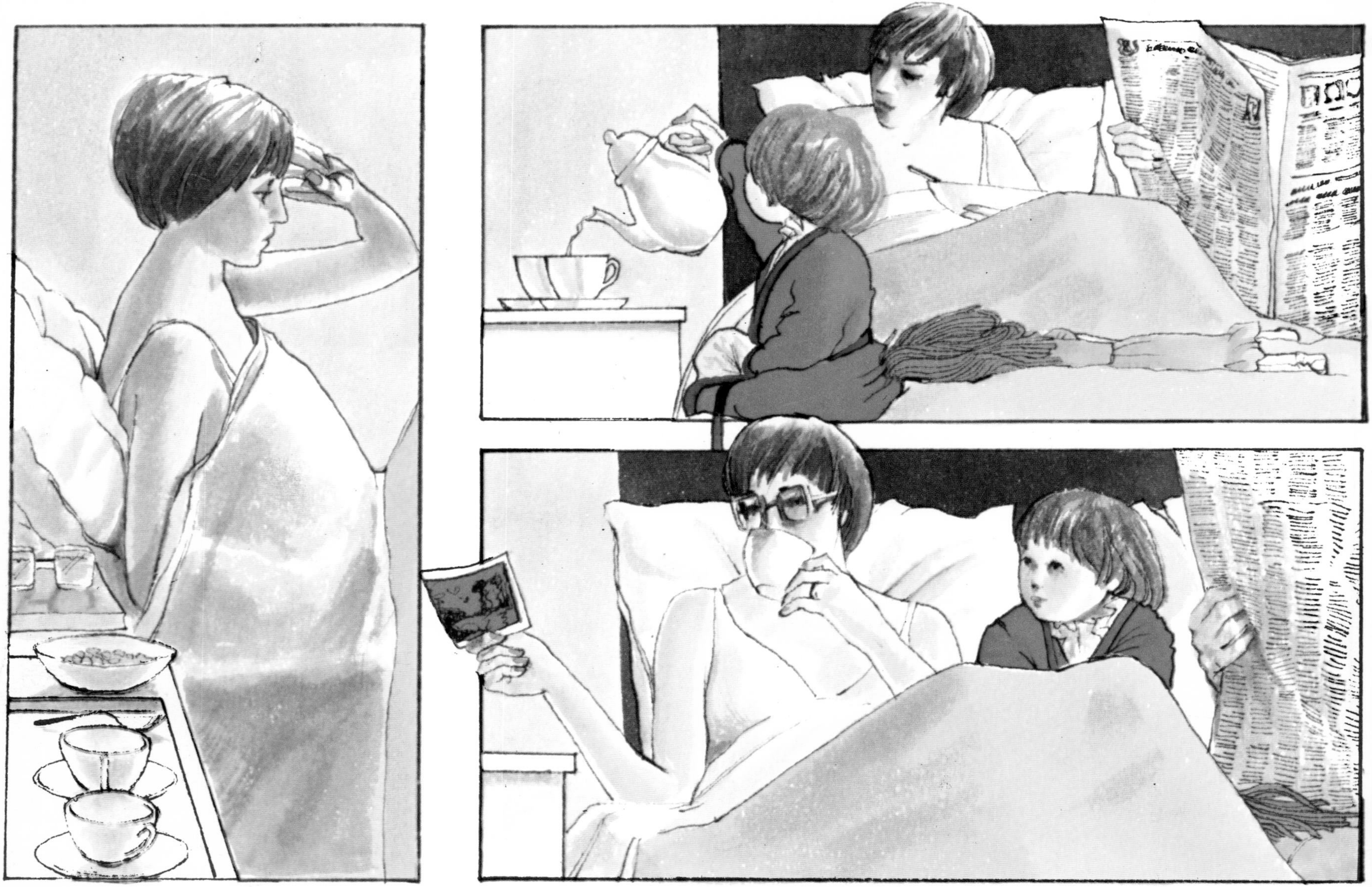

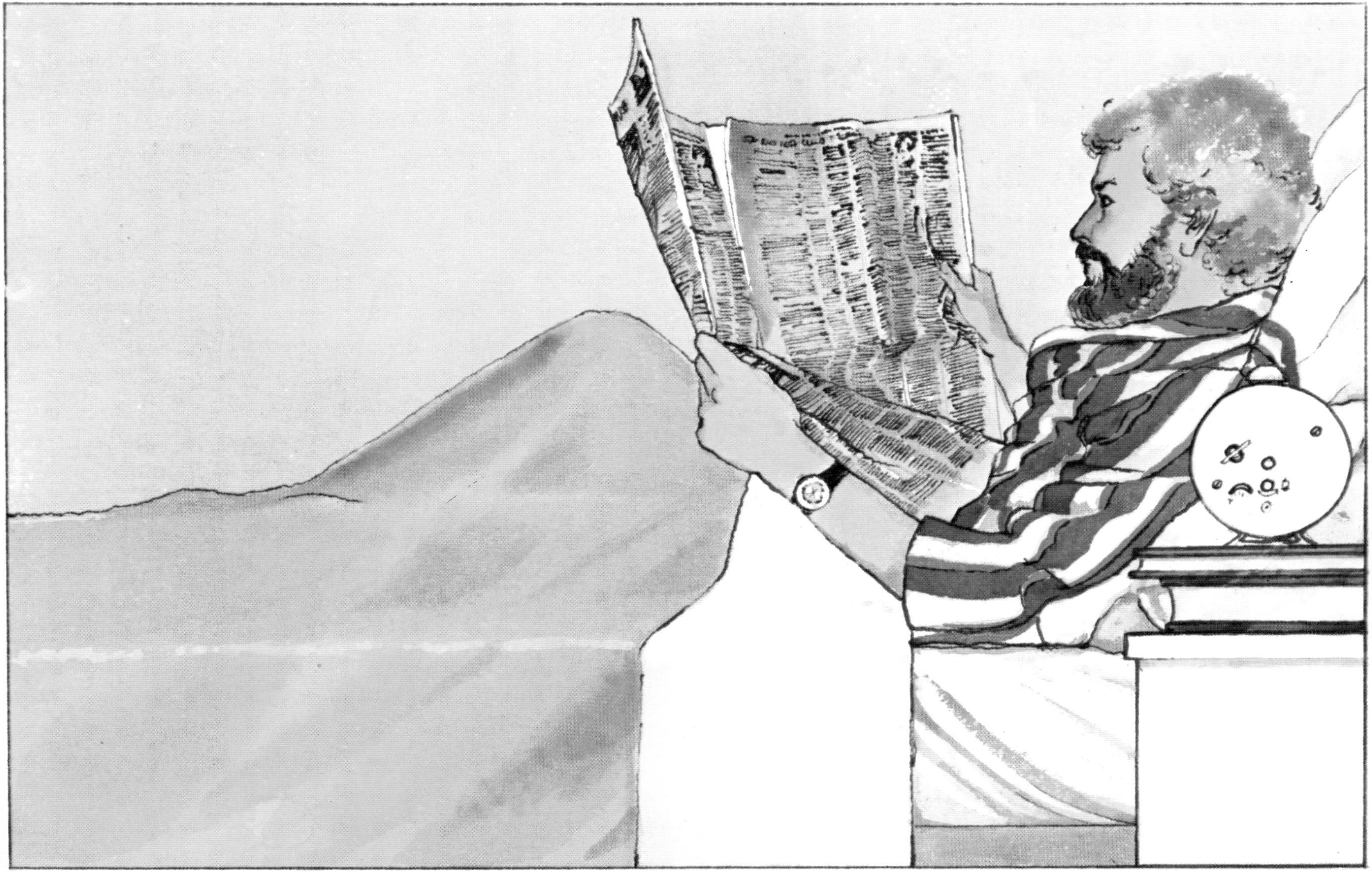

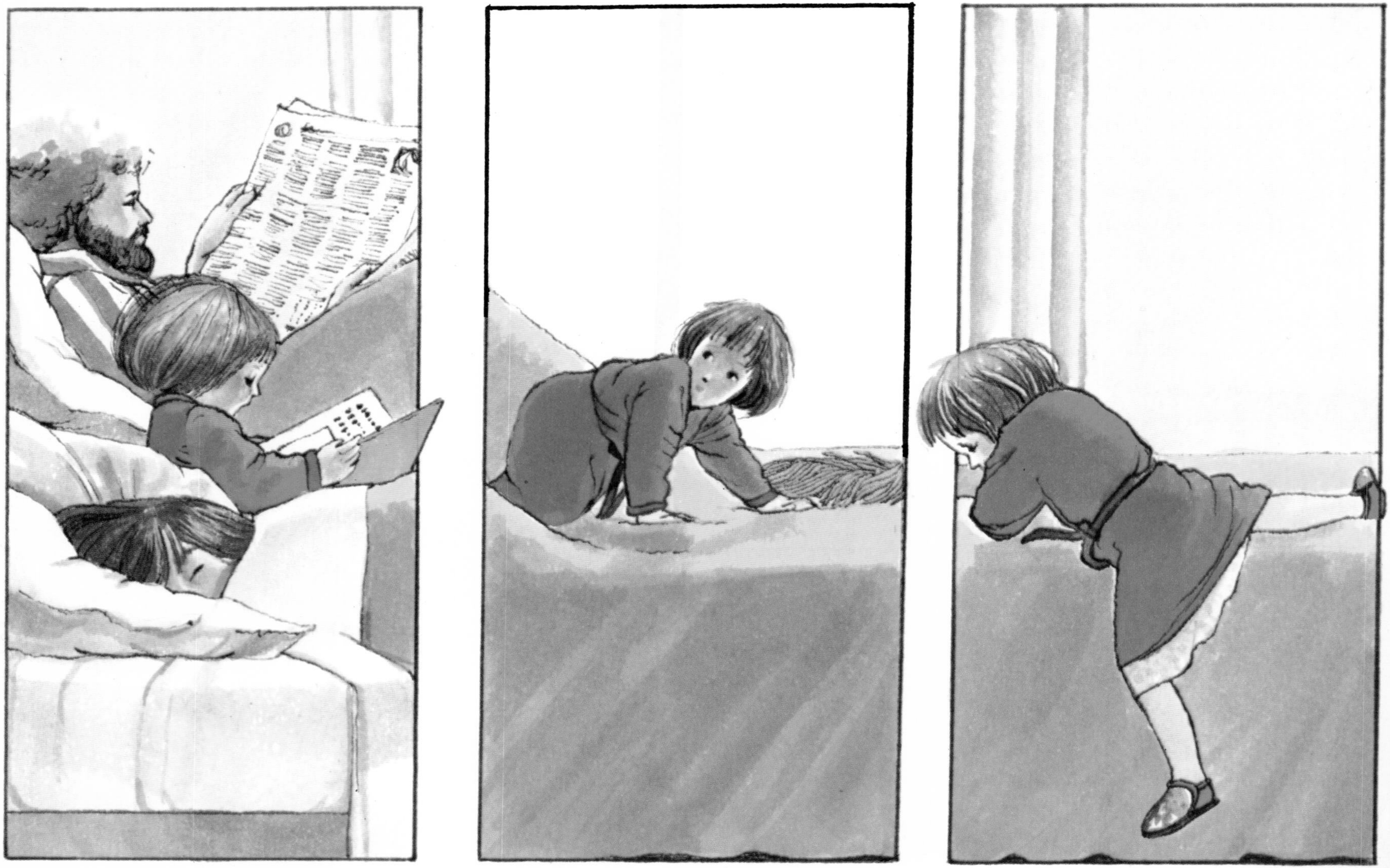

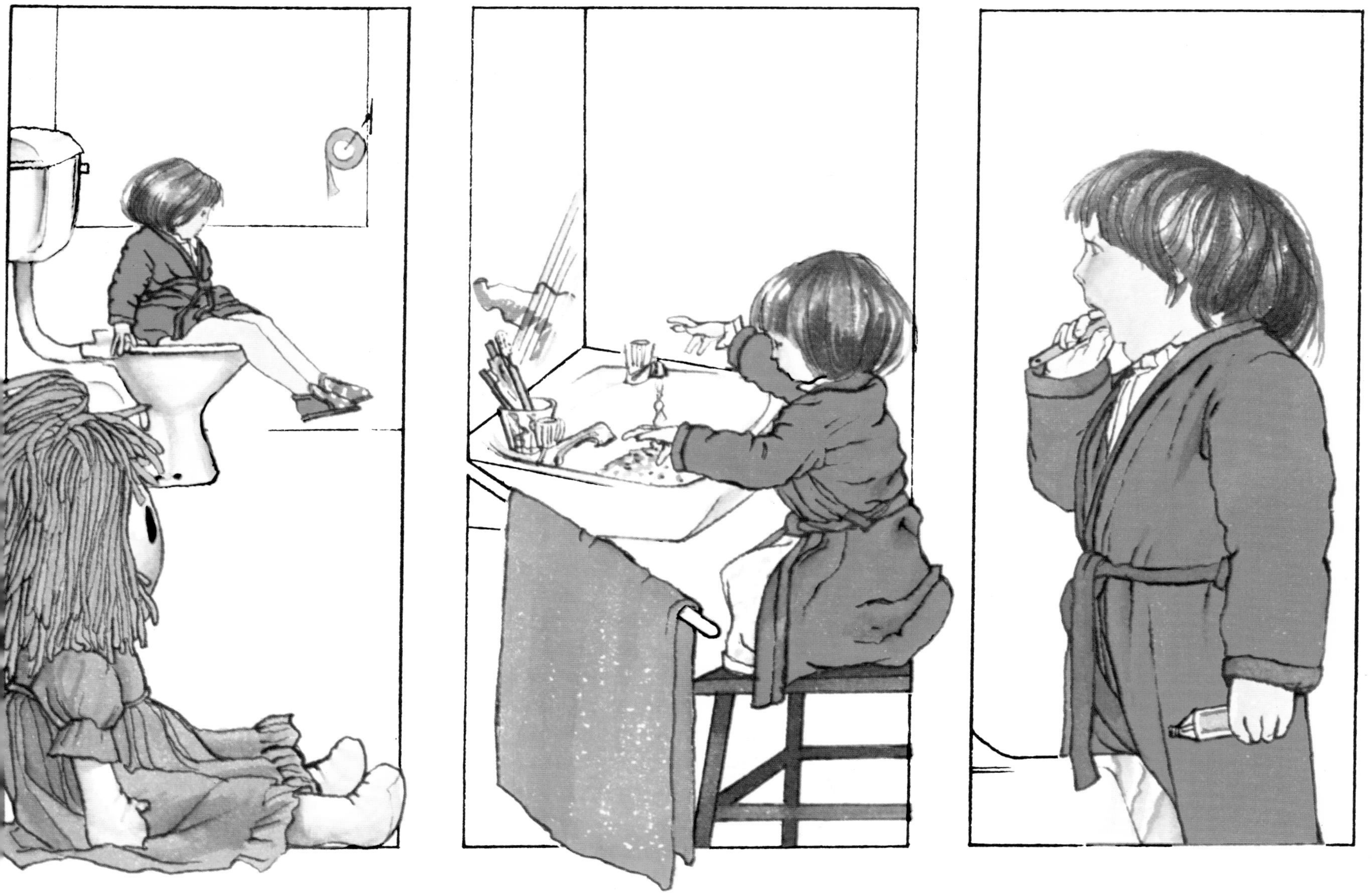

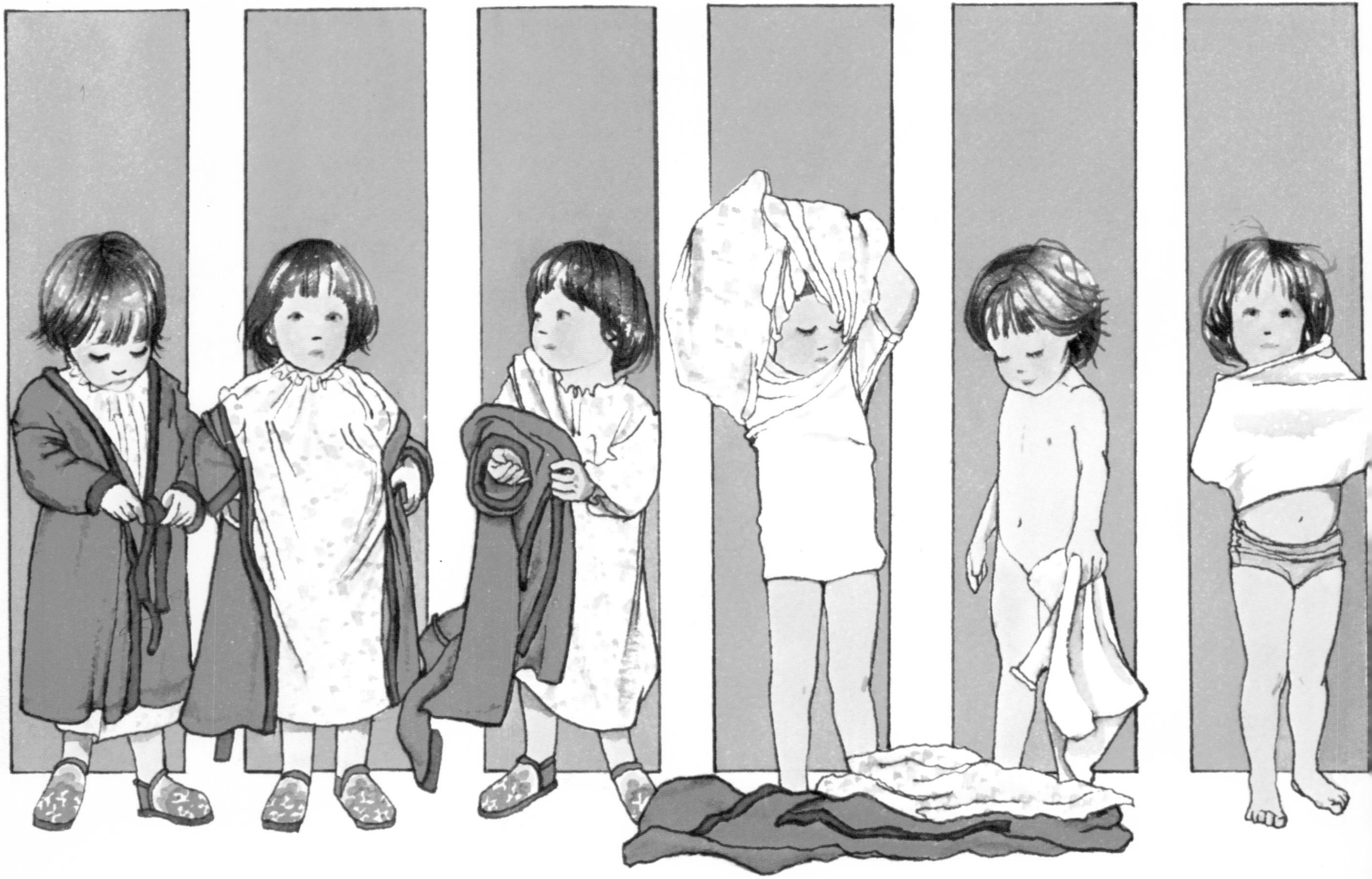

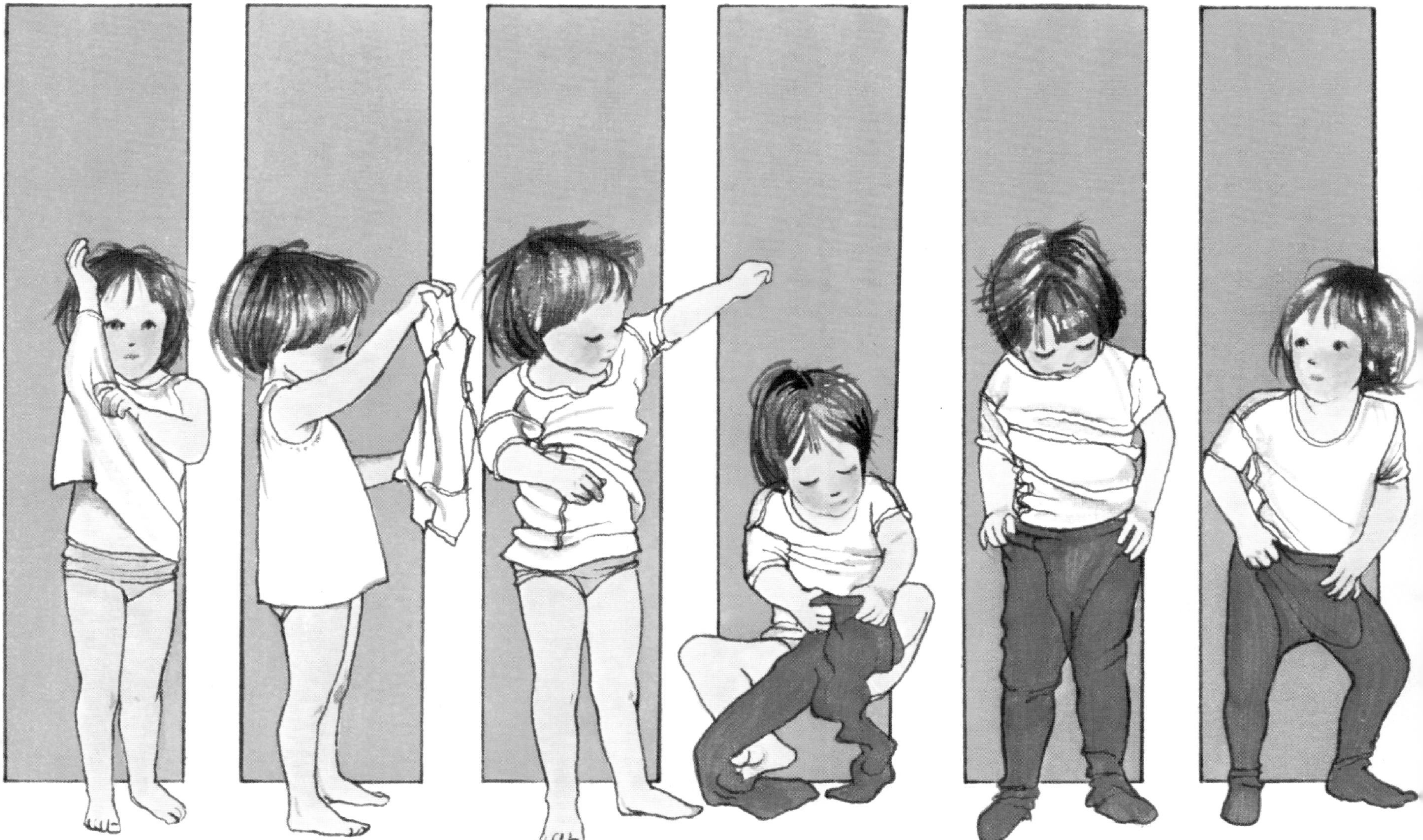

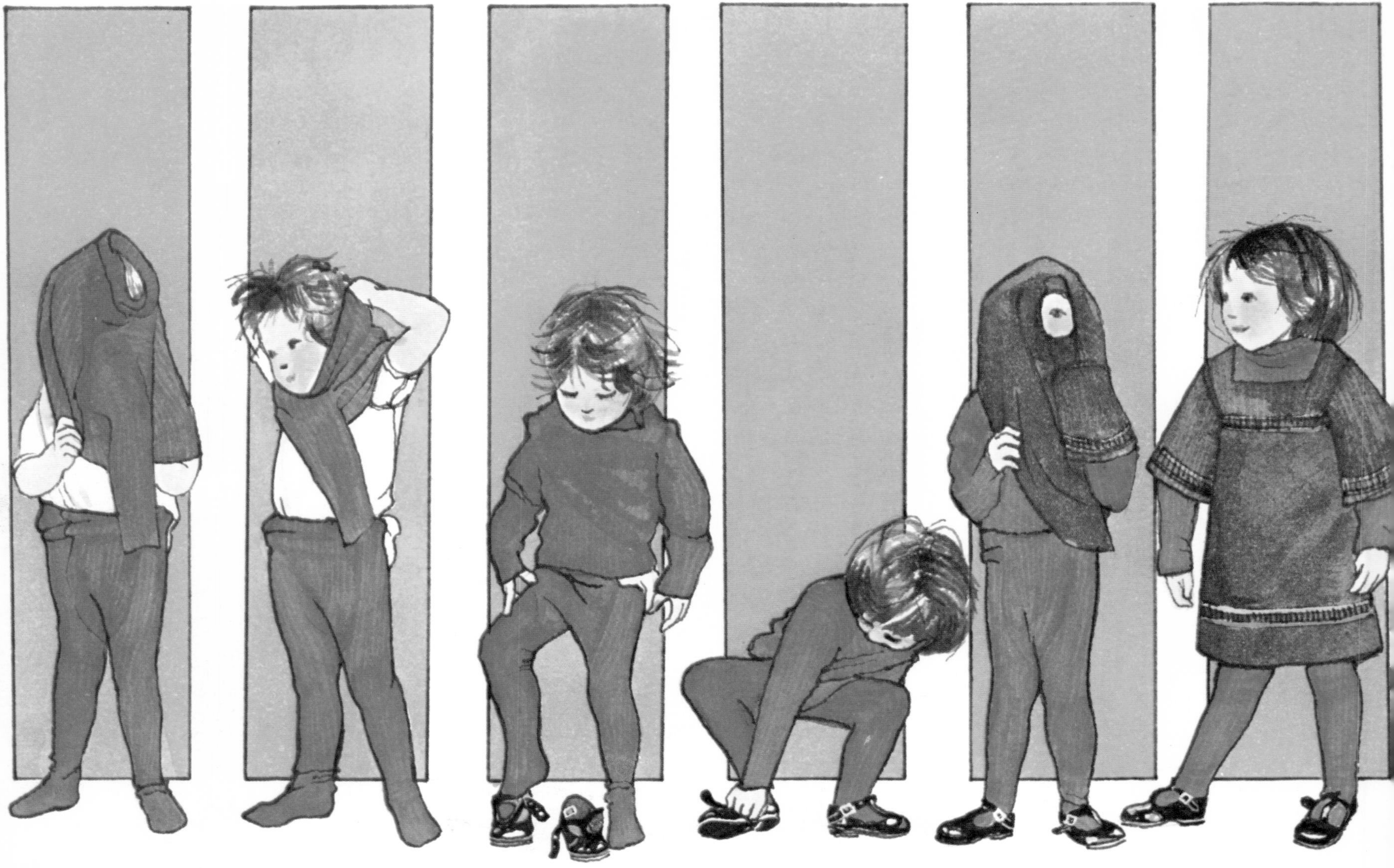

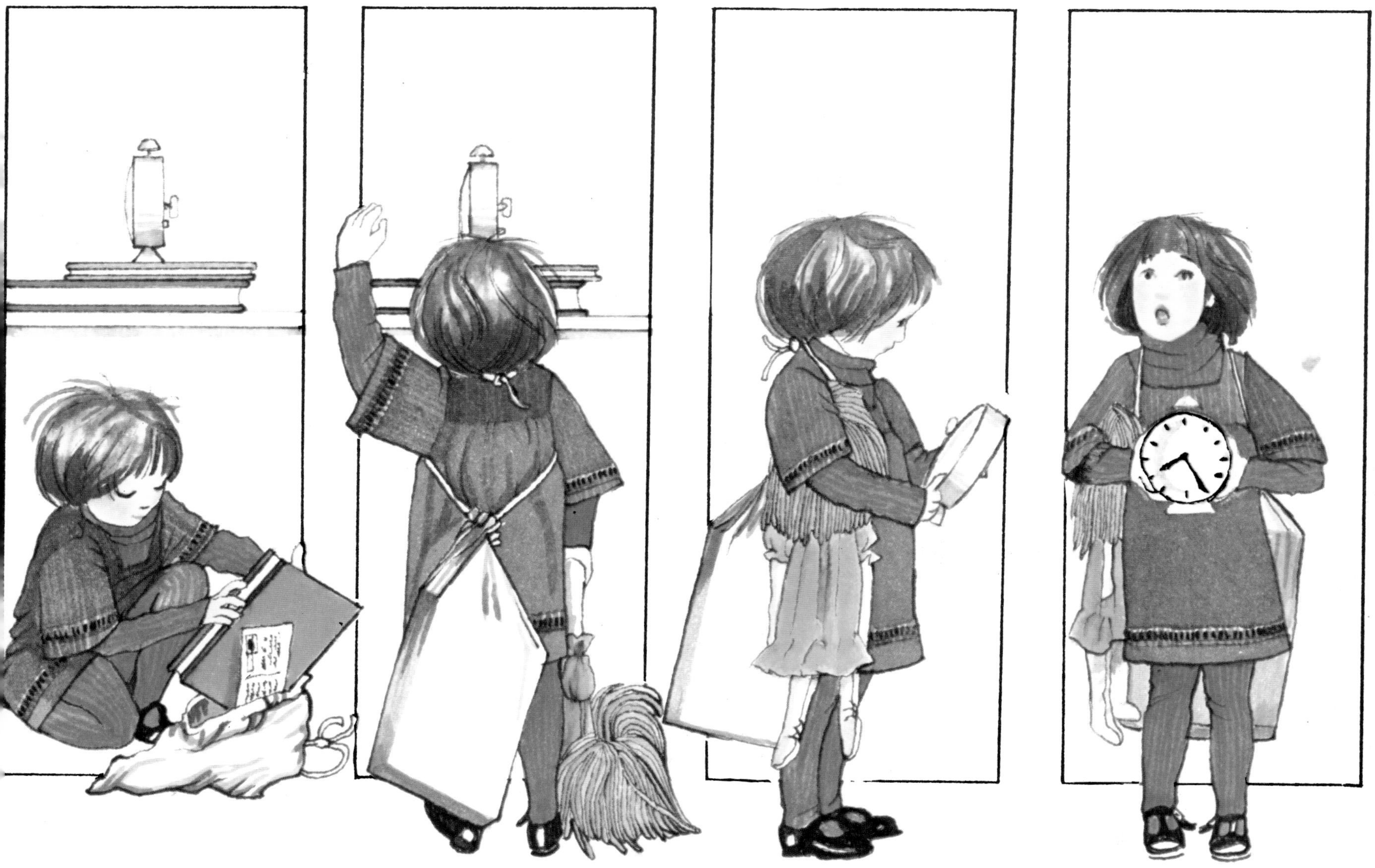

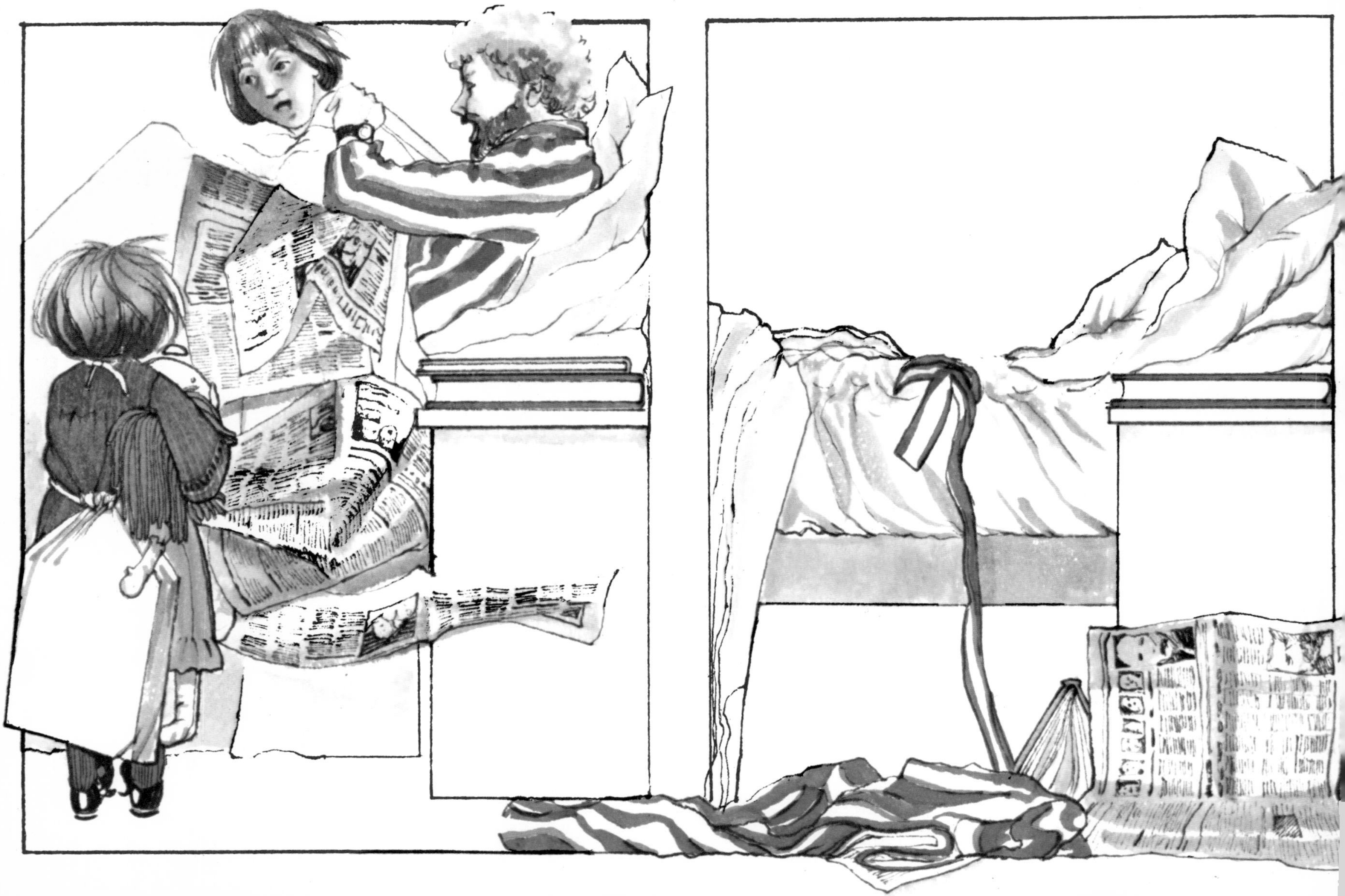

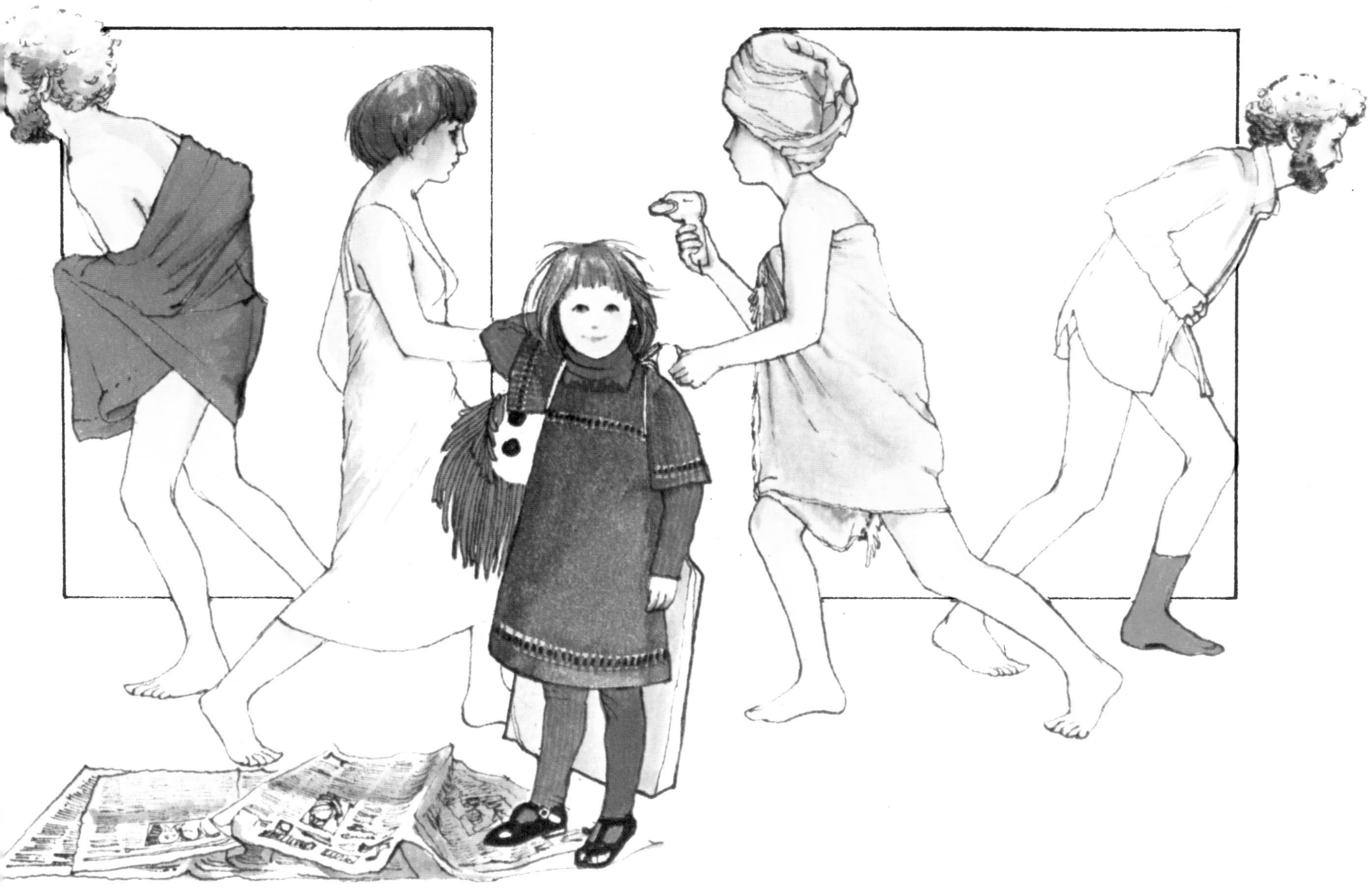

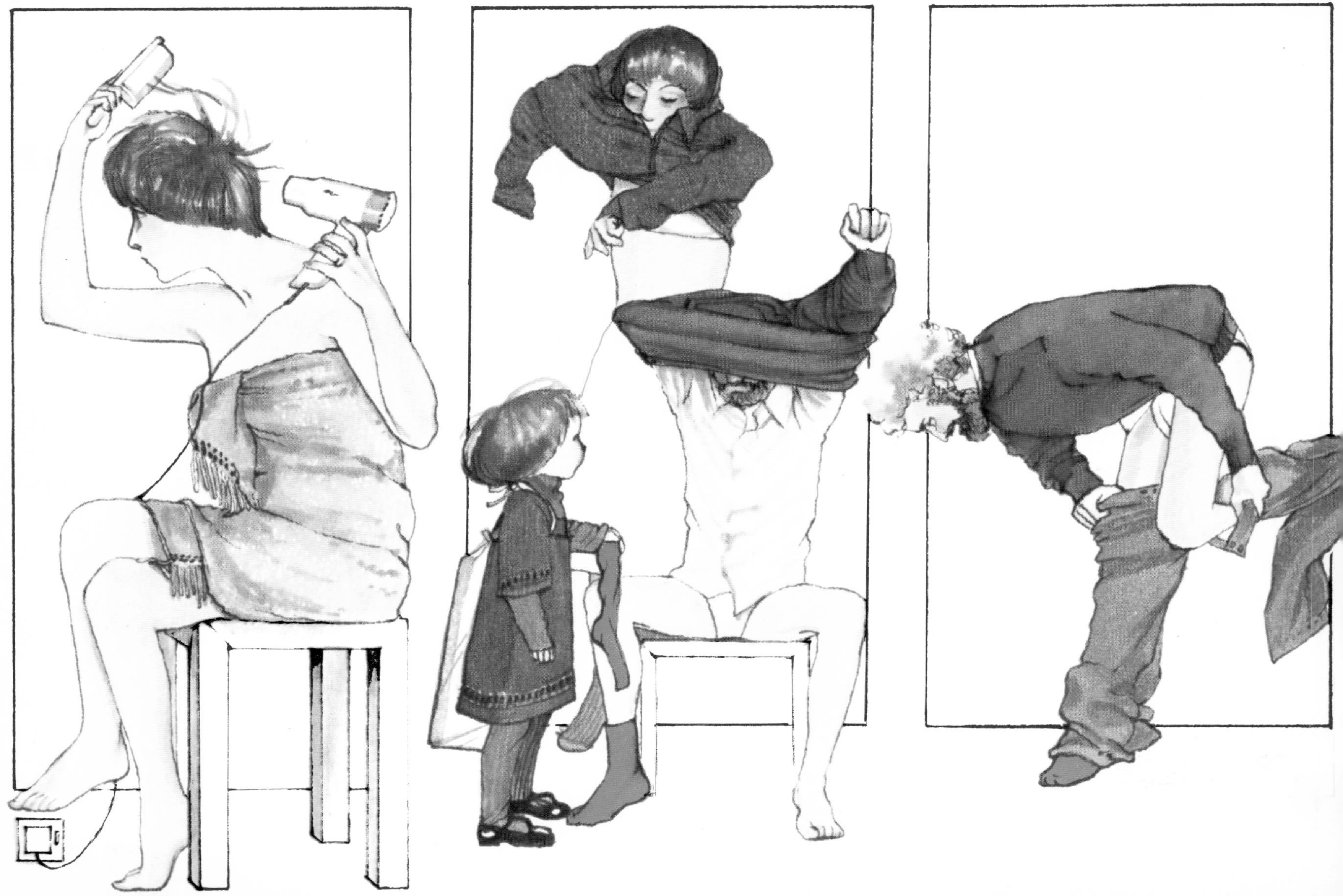

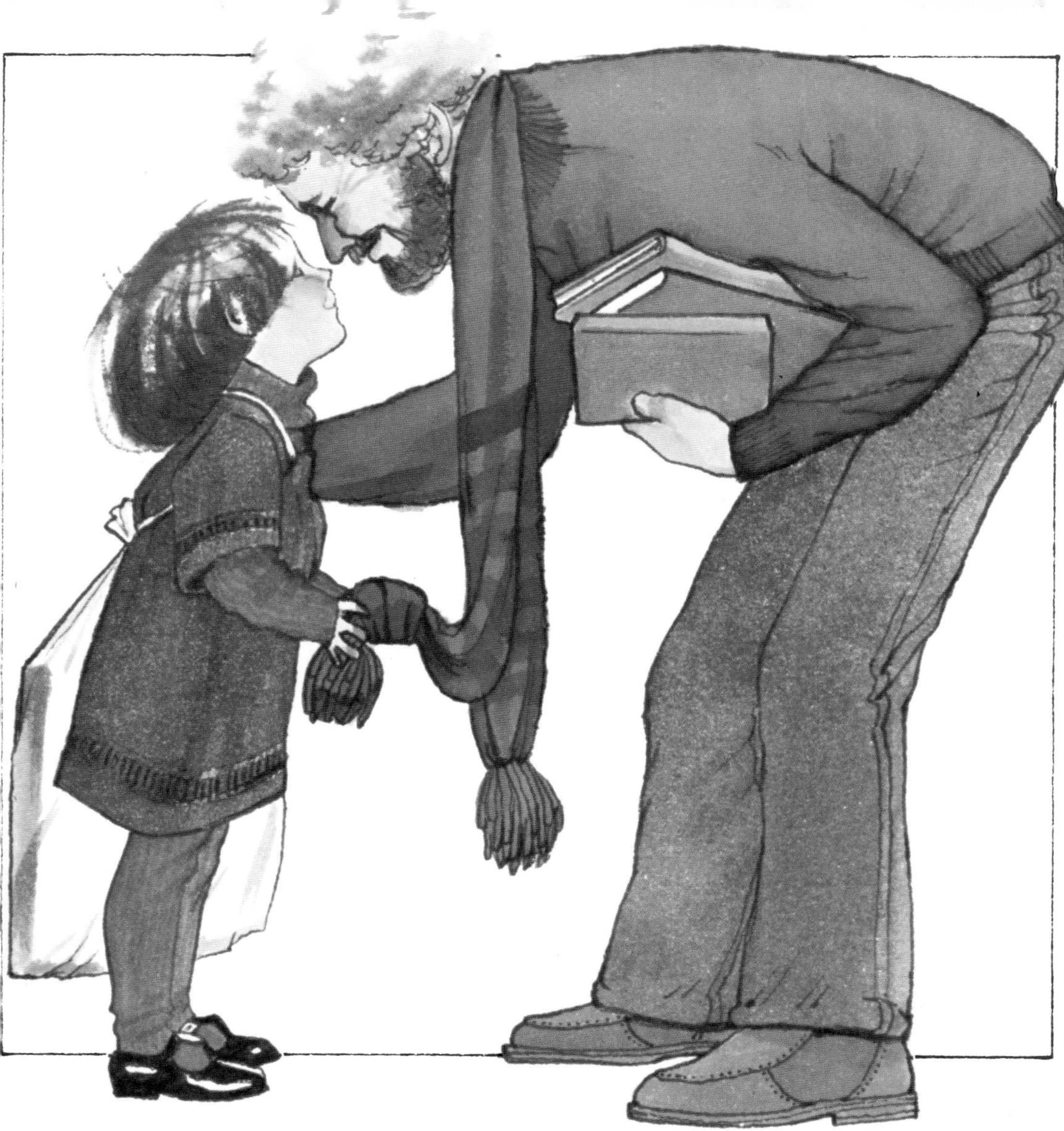
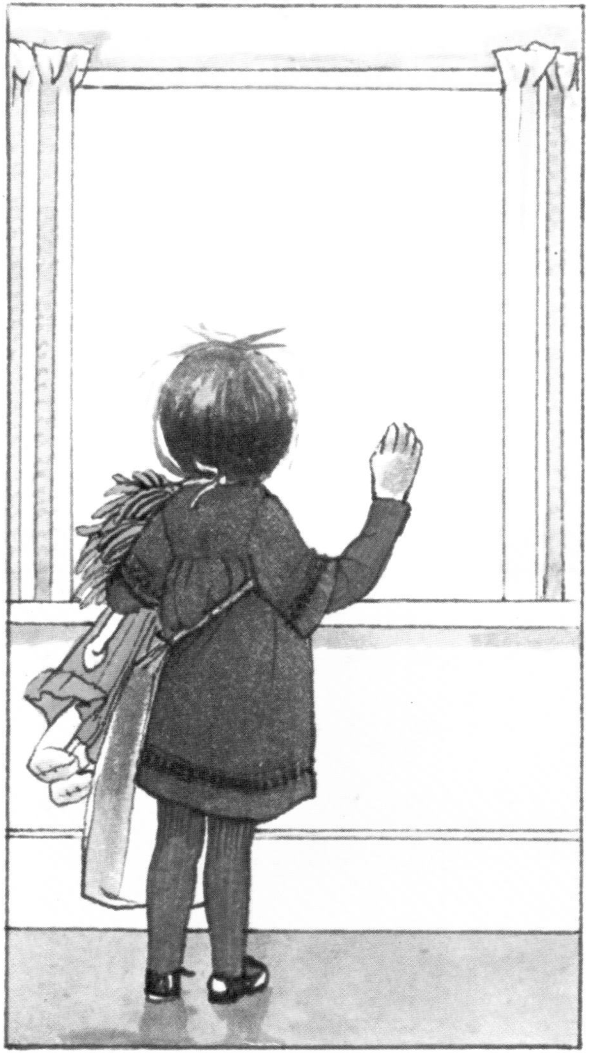

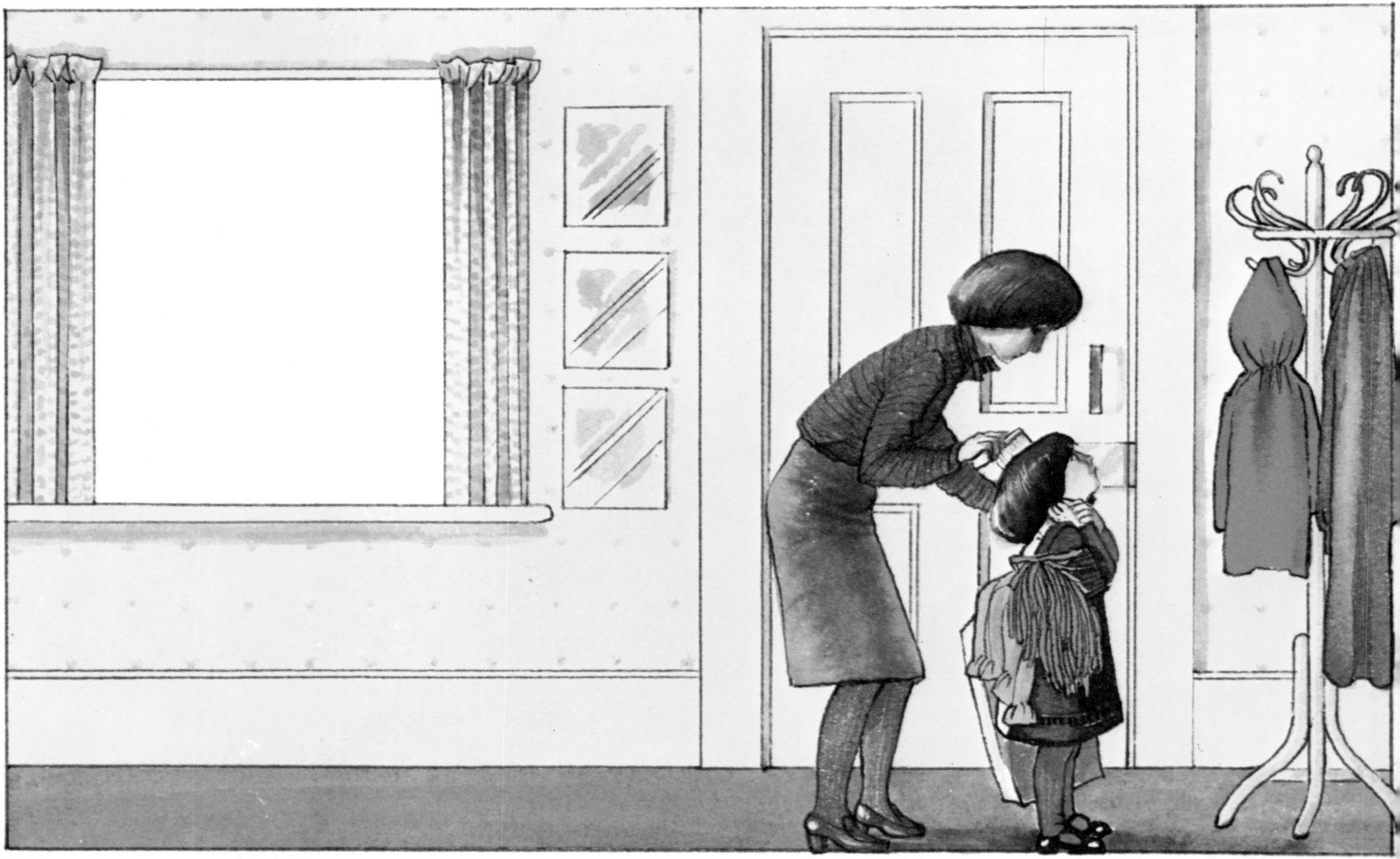

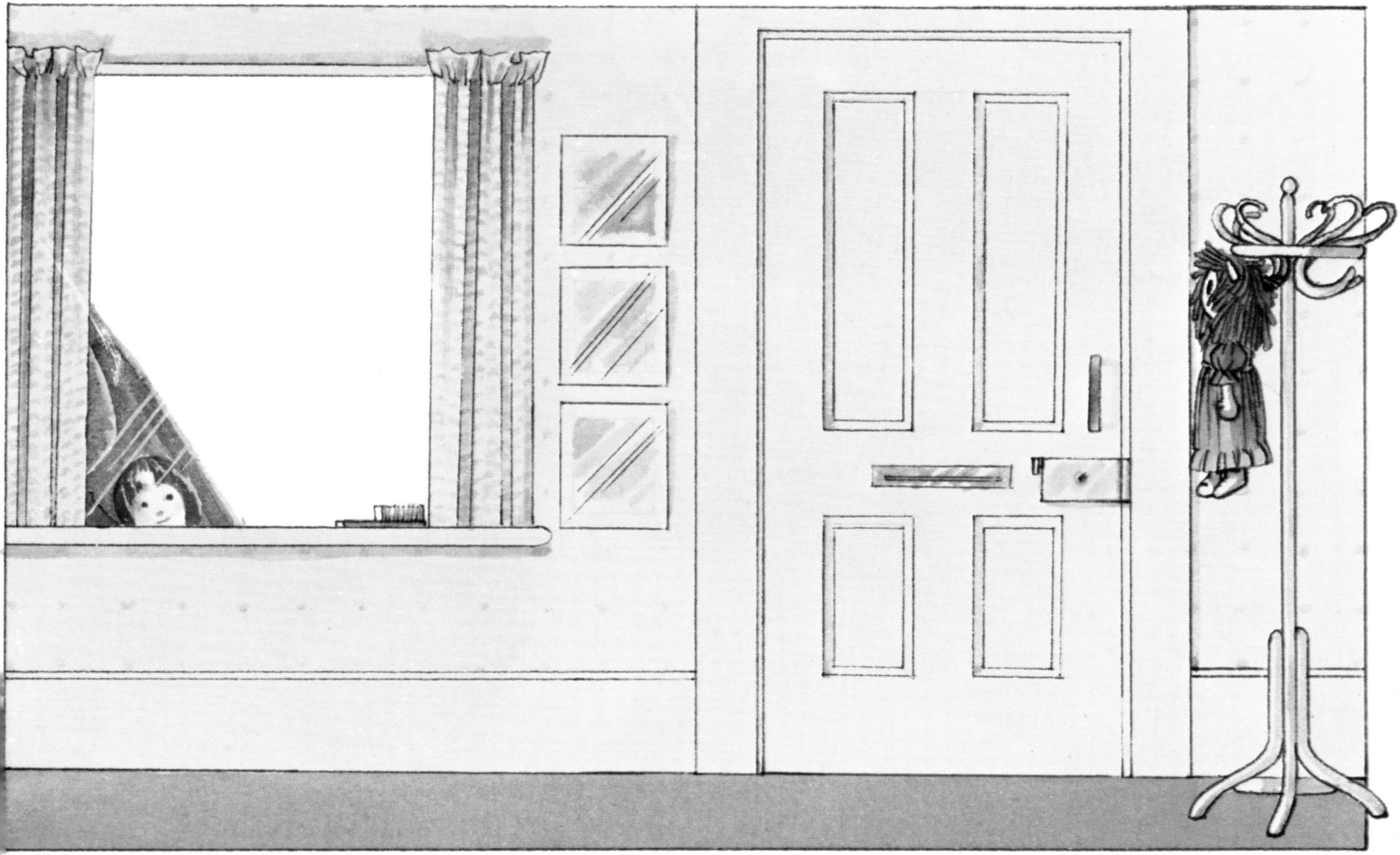

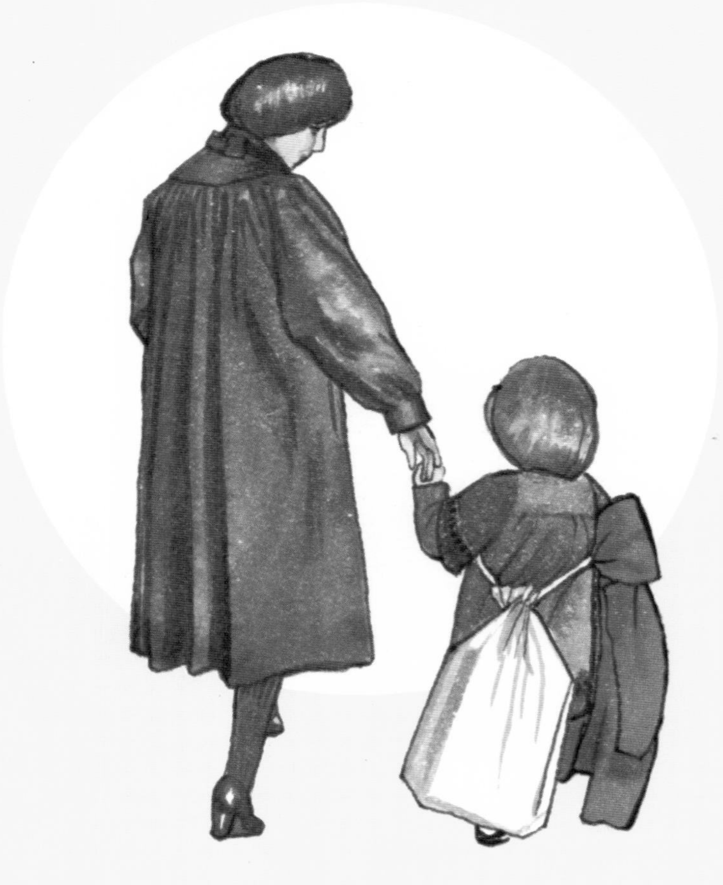